さくらまつ

―夜が明けたら―

もくじ

プロローグ

春に吹く風
雲雀東風

龍が起こす
春疾風

追い風なら
　　走れる、速く

向かい風なら
　　飛べる、遠くへ

風が凪いだら
思い馳せよう
空を仰いで
大切なあの日に

その一　　出会い

松と風が出会ったのは、遠い過去のことでした。

そのころの風は落ち着きがなく、落ち着くつもりもありませんでした。ちいさな花たちをそよそよ口説いては、ふらっといなくなる毎日をくり返し、「人生これでいいやなどと思っていました。そんな風がある春の夜、巨大な嵐と喧嘩して突き飛ばされ、衝突したのが、この若い松だったのです。

松は細身の体で風の衝突をびくともせずに受けとめてみせました。松葉も樹皮も飛び散らかさず、枝ひとつ折れませんでした。

翌朝。夜の嵐にくたびれた周囲の木々の中で、その松だけはひとり、まぶしい朝日に向かってすっくりと背中を伸ばしていました。風が今まで見たこともないすがすがしさでした。

「すごいね」

風は心から言いました。

「まだまだだよ」

松は笑ってさらりとこたえました。ゆうべ自分にぶつかってきた風を責めようともせず、毅然として立っています。そしてあちこち飛びまわっている風を、

8

素直にうらやましがりました。

「いいなあ、お前、いろんなところに行けて」

その言葉は風を不思議な気持ちにさせました。いままで会ったどの木にも感じなかった親しみを、その声から感じ取ったのです。いきなり「お前」と呼ばれたことさえ、うれしく思えました。

風は言いました。

「世界の話なら、いくらでも運んできてやるよ。ちょっと時間をくれたら地球の裏側にも行けるんだから。そのかわり……お願いがあるんだ。ぼくのこと、形にしてくれないかな。だれかが揺れてくれないと、ぼくはここにいるってだれにもわかってもらえないんだ。飛び跳ねても、吼えても、何をしても、ああやって嵐に目をつけられるだけで」

「ほかの木は揺れてくれないってこと？」

「適当にへらへら動くだけだよ。威張ってるヤツばっかりでさ。ぼくのこと、ちゃんと認めてはくれないんだ」

「そうか。いいよ。今やってみようか」

風がためしにひゅーんと舞うと、松は硬い枝をしならせ、松葉をうまいことなびかせてみせました。

風は、自分の気持ちがひとつ残らず伝わったことに驚きました。

「どうしてわかるの?」

「知らない。感じるんだ」

松もまた、まるでずっと前から知り合いだったような懐かしさを、風に抱いていたのです。

こうして、松は枝を揺らして風の存在を示し、風は松に季節や天気の変化、世界の出来事を知らせるようになりました。そして二人はともに、周囲の草木から一目おかれる存在へと成長していったのです。

その二

桜

数十年の月日が過ぎました。風と松は力を合わせて、その土地を豊かにしていきました。たまにとっくみあいの喧嘩もしましたが、本気で憎みあったことなど一度もありません。むしろそれは、ほかの土地から嵐が来たときに備えての力試しになりました。

しかし、風は知らなかったのです。松がかかえはじめたある重大な秘密を。

ある日、なんとなく元気のない松を見て励ましたくなった風は、ほんの遊びのつもりで松の腕にじゃれついてみました。一本気な性格の友人を、風はこうやって何度も笑わせてきたのです。しかしこの日、松の枝はあっけなく折れてしまいました。そして次の瞬間、風は目を疑いました。大木となっていた松の体は、内側から朽ち、空洞と化していたのです。

「これ、どういうこと？」

松はがっくりと肩を落とし、かすれた声でうめきました。

「からっぽなんだ！」

松の声はしだいに大きくなりました。

「からっぽなんだ。からっぽになっちゃったんだよ！」

12

「わかるか、この気持ちがお前にわかるか!?」

激しい言葉とともに、松葉がばらばらと抜け落ちました。こんな松を見るのは、はじめてでした。風はただ震えていました。答えられないことが、またどうしようもなく辛く思えました。

安易に「わかるよ」とは言えませんでした。体を持ったことがない風には、

松がいくらか冷静さを取り戻すと、風は勇気をふりしぼり、ちいさな声でたずねました。

「いつから?」

「少し前だよ」

「なんでこうなっちゃったの?」

「わからない」

「どうして言ってくれなかったの」

「言えないよ、こんなこと」

「これからどうなるわけ?」

「もっと衰えて、朽ちていくんだ」

「そんなの見たくないよ」

「しかたないんだ、運命なら」

今度は風が吹き荒れました。

「かっこつけんなよ！」

「……」

松は黙ってしまいました。

松はその日から心を閉ざしてしまいました。一度閉ざしてしまうと、その扉は、たたいても、たたいても、開きませんでした。嵐にも負けないあの強さが、ひとたびこうなると、鉄のような頑なさに変わってしまうことを風は知りました。

松は日に日に衰えていきます。葉は落ち、枝は折れ、それでも松は黙って運命に耐えているようでした。

どうしたら彼の命を、心を救うことができるだろう。

どうしたら、あの快活ですがすがしい松の姿が戻ってくるのだろう。

14

どうしたら。どうしたら。どうしたら。

何日も考え抜いた末、風は、友人の空洞（くうどう）の中に、黙ってひと粒（つぶ）の種を落としました。

種は、すぐに芽を出しました。幸い、吹き抜けになった天井（てんじょう）や横の穴（あな）から日の光がさんさんと降りそそぎ、雨のめぐみもたっぷりと受けられたので、芽はほどなく若木になりました。

松は、その若木を毎日、不思議そうに眺（なが）めていました。

「君は、だれ？」

松が思いきって聞くと、若木は鈴（すず）をふったような声で答えました。

「桜」

松はすくすくと伸びていきました。

ある気持ちの良い朝、桜は突然（とつぜん）、すいっ、と腕（うで）を伸ばしました。しなやかな腕が、松の体に空（あ）いた穴から、ひゅん、と突（つ）き出ました。

「おいおい」と松は言いました。　桜はおかまいなしに、　太陽に向かってその腕を振りました。

またある日、桜はちいさな葉っぱをちろちろとつけて、松をくすぐりました。

「おいおい」と松は言いました。　桜はおかまいなしに、　葉っぱを揺らしてくすくす笑いました。

風はその様子を見守りながら思いました。

もう自分がつきっきりでいなくても大丈夫だ。　幹の傷みは止まっている。　それに桜は明るくて天真爛漫だ。　自分が笑わせなくても、　松の心は癒される。　自分が気晴らしを考えなくても、　松は好きなだけ愉しいことを見つけられる。

さびしくないと言ったら嘘でした。　でも風は、　松が元気を取り戻しただけで充分幸せでした。　それに今では、　風にも大切な仕事がありました。　年々多くの草木が風の言葉に耳を貸すようになり、　このあたり一帯の季節は、　すべて風の仕切りで進められるようになっていたのです。

風は二人を眺め、大きく深呼吸をすると、次の仕事へと旅立っていきました。

その三

光と影（かげ）

松はかつての雄姿を取り戻しました。もう枝は残っていませんでしたが、その幹はがっしりと桜を守り、朝日に、夕日に輝いています。

松はあらゆることを桜に教えました。

太陽が昇るのは東で、沈むのは西だということ、月にもたくさんの種類があること、星座のこと、季節のこと、生き物たちのこと……。

そうして松から深いいつくしみを受けた桜は、いつしか可憐な花を咲かせるようになり、その枝は「天女の腕」と呼ばれるほどたおやかな色香をたたえるようになりました。

二本の木は、細かいでこぼこも、わずかな傾きも、何もかもしっくり同じでした。同じ鳥の声を聞き、同じ空を見上げ、めざめたときから眠るときまで共にいましたが、それを苦痛に感じることは一度もありませんでした。些細なことでも、言葉がなくなり、眠くなるまで語り合いました。

たまに舞い戻ってくる風の土産話から、二人はいくつもの歌を生み出しました。桜の声は透きとおるように美しく、松の声は生きるものすべてをつつむあたたかさに満ち、その二重唱は風に乗って野をわたり、山をわたり、かなたま

で響いていきました。

でも……。幸せだった松の心にふたたび新たな翳りがさしはじめたのは、人間たちが通りかかり、こんな会話をかわしていった日のことでした。

「これが有名な『さくらまつ』？」

「すごいね、幹が松で枝が桜？」

「でもなんだか桜、窮屈そうじゃん？」

「これじゃあ、あんまり大きくなれないかもね」

大きくなれない……。その言葉は松の心に鋭く突き刺さりました。桜をちらりと見ると、桜は気にもとめず、鼻歌を歌いながら空を見ていました。

松はあらためて桜を見つめなおしました。ほかの桜に比べて、その幹が極端に細いことは確かでした。

陽があたらない分、保たれている繊細な色合い。でもこのままではどう見ても一人で生きていけそうにはない。それはほかでもなく自分のせいだ。自分は桜の未来をさまたげているのだろうか？ 桜自身がまだ気づいていない未来

を。

松は思いました。

「このままじゃだめなんだ」

そして、胸の奥がぎゅっと締めつけられるのを感じました。

「どうしたの？」

歌いやめた桜が、屈託のない表情で松を見つめました。

松は自分の思いを伝えることができませんでした。

そうだ、いつか、なんとかして、人間たちにこの桜を植え替えてもらおう。

でもそれは同時に、桜が自分の毎日から消えてしまうことを意味していました。その笑い声も、いたずらな小枝も、なめらかな幹も、歌も、自分の毎日から消えてしまうことを。想像しただけでも心が引き裂かれそうでした。

松は苦しげに眉をひそめて、桜から目をそむけました。そんな松を見て、桜は発狂せんばかりに気づかいました。

「何かあったの？　具合、悪いの？　どこか痛む？」

桜がまとわりつけばつくほど、松は苦しくなりました。

20

君を縛っているのはこのぼくだ、でも君がいなくちゃ生きていけない、どうしたらいい……。

それらの言葉は、松の喉もとまで出かかっては、ばらばらにはじけていきます。松は今までになく混乱していました。いつになく冷たい松の腕の中で、桜は悲しみにくれていました。どうして桜がそれを理解できるでしょう。でも、

「あんなにわかり合えていたのに……」

深く傷ついたせいで、その春ついた花のつぼみは、いつもよりずっと青白く見えました。

かろうじて花がひらくと、桜は松が眠っているすきに、こっそり風を呼びました。

「どうかしたの？」

「お願いがあるの。私の花、散らして」

「えっ、どういうこと？ 今朝咲いたばっかりじゃない」

「いいから」

桜は頑としてゆずりません。桜は松の言ったことを覚えていました。松は言ったのです、毎年花が重くなるね、と。うれしそうだったけれど、ほんとうは支えるのが辛いに違いない、松の苦痛はそのせいなのだ、と桜は思っていました。

「言えないんだと思うの、私に。でもこのままじゃ、私が松さんの体をだめにしてしまう。だからお願い」

「そんなことできないよ」

「お願い」

桜のあまりに悲痛な表情に、風は気が進まないまま、生まれたばかりの花びらを吹き散らしました。花びらは成熟を待たずにほうぼうに流れていき、花見を楽しみにやってきた人々はがっかりして言いました。

「間に合わなかったねぇ」

「風があったからなあ」

人々はうらめしそうに風をにらみました。

松はその人々をじっと見つめました。そしてしばらくのあいだ封印してい

た、あたたかく穏やかな声で桜をさとしました。

「なぁ、自分が何のために生きているのか、考えたこと、あるか」

「……」

「考えるんだ。そしてもう二度と、こんなことをするんじゃない」

その夜のこと。遠出をしていた風の耳に、異様な音が届きました。松が嵐を呼び寄せたのです。稲妻が空を走り、激しい雨が地をたたきました。強い光を浴びて、木々はまるで色を失ったように白く浮かび上がりました。松は覚悟を決めていました。

今晩、自分を粉々にするのだ。一日も早く、桜を自由の身にしてやるのだ。

光がいよいよ頭上の空を切り裂いたとき、松はカッと眼を見開いてその閃光に身をまかせました。

「さあ、来い。何も怖くはない。ひと息に終わらせろ！」

しかし次の瞬間……松の心臓は凍りつきました。いつのまにか目をさました桜が、嵐に向かって必死に首をもたげ、枝という枝で松をかばっているではあ

りませんか。若葉がはぎとられ、か細い枝が吹き飛びました。松は、声を枯らして風を呼びました。

風が駆けつけたとき、桜は半ば気を失いかけていました。嵐はゴロゴロと悪態をつきました。風は持てる力をすべて爆発させて、嵐を遠ざけました。

「くそったれ、松の野郎が来てくれって言うから来てやったんだ!」

風は松の前に立ちはだかって突っぱねました。

「本気でなんか頼んでねぇよ!」

「このへたれ小僧、いつからそんな口をきけるようになった」

「もうあんたより強いんだよ、わかったらとっとと消えろ!」

嵐は高笑いしながらかなたへと去っていきました。

風がふりかえると、松は黙って桜を抱きしめていました。熱い樹液が松の体をめぐり、それがぐったりした桜をあたためていました。

「いっしょにいよう」

そのひと言を呑み込んで、松は何も言えないまま、ただしっかりと桜を抱きしめていました

その四　　満月

意識を取り戻した桜は、その晩から日夜を問わず考えぬきました。自分の生きる意味を。

なぜ生まれてきたんだろう、

なぜここにいるんだろう、

何のために毎年花をつけるんだろう……。

言葉にこそなりませんでしたが、桜はしだいに感じるようになりました。自分の奥底から、ひとつの決意が湧いてくるのを。それは日々の目覚めを爽やかにさせ、生きるエネルギーとなり、夜の眠りを安らかにしました。

そして翌年。春の知らせを受けた桜がまとった花々の、なんと美しかったことでしょう。それはほかの山からのぞきにやってきた春風たちが動きを止めてしまうほどの艶やかさでした。

松はそんな桜をほれぼれと眺めました。

風が松にささやきました。

「すごいよ、どこの桜より見事だ」

26

くっきりした満月が空に現れました。

松のしかかる重みを全身で支えながら、そっと桜をめで、低い声でつぶやきました。

「きれいだ」

桜は目を閉じてそのぬくもりを感じていました。

月は、空高くのぼっていきます。

松は、月と花々をまぶしそうに見上げました。

「明日も、晴れるな」

「うん、きっと晴れる」

静かでした。

松の頭には、ある情景が夢のように浮かんでいました。そして

「夜が明けたら……」

そう言いかけたとき。

松はふと、異変を感じました。一本のヒビが、静かに、静かに、自分の体を這っていきます。

「これは……」

悪夢の予感をともなったそのヒビが体の半ばに達した瞬間、激しい痛みがつらぬきました。松は苦痛のあまり身をよじりました。桜の鋭い叫び声が聞こえました。足元が土を跳ね上げて浮き上がりました。全力で踏ん張っても、花の重みで耐えることができません。松はそのまま傾いていきました。

桜は目をぎゅっと閉じ、自分の足元がぎりぎりと裂けていく痛みを、歯をくいしばって受け止めていました。

「来てしまったんだ、この時が、来てしまったんだ」

動転する気持ちをおさえつけ、桜は必死に自分に言い聞かせました。

「ゆっくり、倒れるなら、松さんの体が地面に打ち付けられないように、せめてゆっくり……」

桜は松にほほを寄せました。樹液をはげしく流し、熱した自分の体で、いままで自分を支えてきた松の体をあたためようとしました。

松は桜に寄りかかりました。何年も抱きつづけてきた桜の幹が、ひときわやわらかく、豊かで、安らぎに満ちているのを感じながら。

こうして満月の下で、満開の花をつけたまま、二人はゆっくりと倒れ(たお)ていきました。

「倒れたぞ、松と桜が心中(しんじゅう)したぞ」

町中にそんなうわさが駆(か)けめぐりました。人々がわらわらと集まり、言葉もなく立ち尽(つ)くしました。大地一面にたっぷりと咲(さ)き乱れた、うす紅色の花々。ほの明るく月光をまとい、かぐわしい香りを放っています。その光景に人々はただ打たれていました。

満月はすべてを見下ろしながら、ゆっくりと空を渡(わた)っていきました。長い時がたち、ひとり、またひとりと、人々の姿が消えていきます。月は、松と桜を照らし続けました。松がそっと、その呼吸を止めるまで。

やがて……。桜は、白くけぶった朝もやの中で目を開けました。小鳥の声が遠くに聞こえ、アリが数匹(すうひき)、体の上を這(は)いまわっていました。

風がしずかに花びらをなでていました。

「気がついた？」

風に聞かれ、桜は、かすれた声でたずねかえしました。

「……あの人は？」

風は答えました。

「死んだよ」

それ以上、何が言えたのでしょう。

そしてその言葉は、かみしめてしまったらきっと立ち直れなくなる。

風は言葉の余韻を待たずにたずねました。

「痛む？」

桜は答えませんでした。そして堰を切ったようにむせび泣きました。

風の心にやるせない思いがこみあげました。自分もどこかが痛かったらいいのにと。涙で草木を濡らし、地面を足で叩けたならと。何十年もの間、同じ時をわかちあってきたかけがえのない友とは、もう、口をきくこともできないのです。

風は身をひるがえして山のかなたへ飛び、荒れに荒れました。龍の棲む、い

にしえの野山に生まれ、体を持たず、ゆえに、痛みも、涙も、命の終わりも知らぬ自分が許せないまま。

ふと、声がしました。

「久しぶりだな、小僧」

「嵐か！　なんで今ごろここにいる」

「辛いか」

「聞くな！」

さえぎるように叫んだ風を、嵐は鋭く一喝しました。

「いいか、どんなに辛くても、目をそらすな、耳をふさぐな。

地上でおきる出来事を、見逃すことなく人々に語りつげ。

大事なときにいなくなるな！」

「どうしてそんなことを」

嵐の声が丸くなりました。

「それが俺たちの役割だからだ。風に生まれるとはそういうことだ。

お前もいつか、わかる日が来る」

その五

鼓動(こどう)

ひとりぼっちになった桜は、しばらくぼんやりと空を見ていました。

「夜が明けたら……」

その言葉の行方(ゆくえ)を、桜は何度もまさぐりました。

松さんは何を言いたかったのだろう、

せめてその答えだけでも聞きたかった。

体をつつんでいる松の木はそのままなのに、そこからはぬくもりが消えていました。すべてが夢のようでした。

「このまま私も死ねたらいいのに……」

そうつぶやいてまぶたを閉じようとしたそのとき。桜の目に映ったのは、う

ている花々。その花びらのひとつひとつに、しっとりとやわらかい生命(いのち)をふく

す紅色の花々でした。いつものように空を背景にではなく、大地を背景に咲い

んで。

桜は、一年かけて見出(みいだ)した答えを……なぜ生まれてきたのか、なぜここにい

るのか、何のために毎年花をつけるのか、その答えを少しずつ思い出しました。

「生きなきゃ……」

桜は思いました。そして弱々しく深呼吸をしました。まだひらいていなかったつぼみがいくつか、少しだけほころびました。腕を伸ばしました。激しい痛みに襲われましたが、草を湿らせた朝露に癒され、土の匂いに励まされました。今まで空ばかり見ていて、忘れていた匂いでした。思えば、この大地に根を下ろして生きてきたのです。松とわけあったのは、最後の痛みだけではありません。この大地こそ、長年、松と桜をつないでくれたものだったのです。

朝の光があたたかく花々にあたりました。

体に少しだけ力を入れました。つぼみが二つ、しめつけていた腕をほどくように、ふんわりとひらきました。

もう少し力を入れてみました。三つのつぼみがひらきました。

さらにもう少し。今度は五つのつぼみがひらきました。樹液が少しずつ、いつもの熱さをとりもどして体を流れていくのを感じました。

「生きなきゃ」

桜は、そして、はっきりと目を開けました。

桜は生き返りました。人々が、折れた根元に土をかぶせてくれたおかげで、体の傷も少しずつ癒えていきました。

夏を乗り切り、秋を過ごし、冬を越しました。

風もまた、そこにいました。桜の気持ちをひきたてようと、あるときはおどけ、あるときはくすぐり、あるときは黙ってそばにいました。かつて松にそうしてきたように。

そして次の春。桜は大地に倒れたまま、ふたたび見事な花を咲かせました。

「おお、これが、『さくらまつ』ですか」

夜桜を見にやってきた見物客が足を止め、連れに向かって問いかけました。

「まだまだ艶っぽいですなあ」

風が桜をつつきます。

「まだまだ艶っぽい、だって」

桜はやれやれと首を振りました。

連れが答えました。

「風がなくて、今日はゆっくり楽しめますなあ」

今度は桜が風に耳打ちします。

「風がなくて、だって」

風が笑いをかみころしました。

人間たちは、しみじみと言いました。

「生きる力、もらいますなあ」

「そうですなあ」

あの日から一年。

今年もまた、丸い月が空高くのぼりました。

風はふと、あの言葉をつぶやきました。

「夜が明けたら……」

その瞬間、風の脳裏に、はじめて出会った翌朝の松の姿がくっきりとよみがえりました。風は松が何を見たかったのか、わかるような気がしていました。

「そう、きっとそうだ」

翌朝。

満月が雲を連れ去り、空は青く澄み渡りました。

風は近くに住む人々の家の窓をたたき、それらが開いたことを知ると、ひと

つ大きくうなずいて桜を見ました。桜もうなずき、そして目を閉じ、すべてを

風にゆだねました。

風は、みずみずしい花びらを渾身の力で舞い上げました。

青空を埋め尽くす、うす紅色のしぶき。

だれも見たことがないほどの、花びらの乱舞。

「見えるか？」

風は叫びました。

「世界一の花吹雪だ！」

花びらは風の中で舞い続けました。

舞い続けて、

38

さくらまつ ──夜が明けたら──

舞い続けて、
天まで舞って、
人々の目に忘れえぬ絶景を残し、
そしてゆっくりと、松の体へ舞い降りていきました。

エピローグ

抱かれるばかりだった桜は、いま無数の花びらで松を抱いています。

天女のようなたおやかさと、母のような慈愛をたたえながら。

そして、旅立つ決心をしました。

風は笑って、いく枚かの花びらをふいっと吹きました。

桜は答えました。

「じゃあね」

「元気で」

「また、来年」

「ええ、また来年」

二人の声が、力強く、春の空にこだましました。

「夜が明けたら！」

あとがき

　その特異な木に出会ったのは、一九九六年四月のある夜のこと。私は京都の上七軒にあった萬春さんにいました。萬春さんは、お茶屋さんを改装して造られたフレンチ・洋食のレストランで、文化芸術関係の人々も多く訪れ、そこにはこれからはばたく若者たちを応援するあたたかい空気が満ちてもいました。

　そんな中、常連らしきお客さまが入っていらして「松と桜が心中しはった」と。私はよほど不思議な顔をしていたのでしょう、オーナーのかよ子さんに、「ほんなら、今から見に行ったらええわ」と促され、写真家の松尾弘子さんに、その「桜松」があるという京都御苑に連れて行っていただきました。そこで目にしたのは衝撃的な光景でした。根こそぎ倒れた木。幹は松、枝は桜。そして見上げるはずの花々が、足元にほの明るく、散らばるように咲いていました。ゆっくり聞いてようやくわかりました。空洞化していたクロマツの上部の虚にヤマザクラの種が落ち、根を下ろして育ったとのこと。それが花をつけたまま倒れ

たのです。松は推定樹齢百年。桜は推定樹齢四十年。春の夜風の中で胸がしめつけられ、「何か書かなければ」という思いに駆られましたが、すぐに形にすることはできず、十年ほどの歳月をかけてゆっくりとこの物語を紡いできました。嬉しかったのは、その間に、もう死んでしまうと思われた桜松が、人々に見守られ、見事な復活を果たしたことでした。

さらに十年ほどたった二〇一六年の春。舞台音楽家の福井小百合さんがこの話を読んで朗読音楽劇にしようと言ってくださいました。そこで歌詞も含めた脚本に書き換え、福井さんの作曲・演奏、演出家の板垣恭一さんのご協力を得て、二〇一七年十月に上演しました。場所は両国のカフェ、black Aさん。キャストには、法月康平さん、皆本麻帆さん、小林タカ鹿さん、tekkanさんが参加してくださり、おかげさまで多くの反響をいただきました。この上演が原作出版への背中を押してくれたことは言うまでもありません。また推敲にあたり、ほんの少し上演版を反映させてもいます。

桜松は、二〇二〇年四月現在も健在で、たくさんの美しい花をつけました。倒れた日から二十年以上の月日を経て、その姿はさらに変化しています。幹は苔むし、その幹から出た枝々は、それぞれが高く空へと向かい、その上部には

桜松。2018年3月末に撮影。

飛び上がってももう届きません。中にはすでに第二の幹のように太くなり始めている枝さえあり、不屈の生命力と尊厳に満ちています。

文章から自由に感じていただきたく、挿絵などは入れていませんが、これを手にとってくださる皆さまの心に何かが伝わり、花ひらけば嬉しく思います。

また、英語に翻訳することでより多くの方に読んでいただけたらという企画を、優れた俳優でもある岩崎MARK雄大さんが叶えてくださいました。この物語では、登場人物たちの性を限定していません。話し方やいくつかの形容から想起されやすい性はあると思い

ますが、大切なのはそれぞれの内面と関係性だからです。岩崎さんもこの趣旨に賛同して、翻訳を進めてくださいました。英文で描かれる世界も、併せてお楽しみいただければ幸いです。

最後になりましたが、この本を出版するにあたり、ご尽力くださった銀の鈴社の阿見みどりさま、西野真由美さま、西野大介さま、英訳してくださった岩崎ＭＡＲＫ雄大さま、ご縁をつくってくださった島崎亮平さま、作品が歩き出すきっかけをくださった福井小百合さま、貴重なアドバイスをくださった板垣恭一さま、作品を輝かせてくださったキャストやスタッフの方々、京都で桜松とのご縁を作ってくださり、私の活動を応援してくださっていた故・松尾弘子さま、故・伊藤かよ子さま、ご協力くださった小澤智子さま、菊地かなえさま、今は亡き最愛の両親、そして、支えてくださった多くの皆さまに、心より感謝いたします。

令和二年春

白石 和己

白石 和己（しらいし わき）

東京生まれ。聖心女子大学英文科卒業。イギリス留学、広告会社勤務などを経てフリーとなり、童話、随筆、詩、脚本、取材記事などを執筆。著書に『京都 能と花の旅』（檜書店）、『五十嵐文男の華麗なるフィギュアスケート』（新書館）他。原作提供・脚本にアプローチシアター『旅の用意ができたよ』、SWays Project『さくらまつ』他。月刊『パセオ・フラメンコ』誌に随筆と童話『和己も歩けば……フラメンコの森で』を連載。

岩崎MARK雄大（いわさき マーク ゆうだい）

米国出身。東京大学文学部英文科卒業。幼少期をアメリカで過ごした英語ネイティブ。俳優（Theatre Company カクシンハン所属）としてシェイクスピアを現代的に演出した舞台で活動する傍ら、海外アーティストとの公演・ワークショップの通訳、戯曲や詩、小説などの翻訳も多数行う。また、イングリッシュ・コーチとして子供から大人まで幅広く英語を指導している。

Twitter: @yudaimiwasaki

Waki Shiraishi

Born in Tokyo. Graduate of the University of the Sacred Heart, Tokyo, Department of English, Communication and Cultures. After studying abroad in the UK and working for an advertising agency in Tokyo, she became a freelance writer, writing fairy tales, essays, poems, scripts, and interview articles. Her works include *KYOTO: A journey of noh and flowers* (published by Hinoki Shoten, Co., Ltd.) and *Fumio Igarashi's Glorious Figure Skating* (published by Shinshokan Co., Ltd.). She has written the original plot and script *We're Ready for the Trip* for Aproach Theatre, and *SakuraMatsu* for SWays Project, and others. She is writing a series of short stories/essays "If Waki walks...in the forest of Flamenco" in the magazine *Monthly Paseo Flamenco*.

Yudai Mark Iwasaki

Raised in North America. Graduate of the University of Tokyo, Faculty of Literature. Native English speaker, brought up in the United States. Performs contemporary style Shakespeare as an actor on stage (member of Theatre Company Kakushinhan), while also translating for foreign artists in international productions/workshops, and translating scripts, poems, and novels. Also is popular as an English coach for children to adults.

Ami; Ms. Mayumi Nishino and Mr. Daisuke Nishino of Ginnosuzusha Co., Ltd., who helped me publish this book; Mr. Yudai Mark Iwasaki for the English translation; Mr. Ryohei Shimazaki for introducing me to the publisher; Ms. Sayuri Fukui for creating the opportunity for the story to take its first baby steps; Mr. Kyoichi Itagaki for his precious advice; every member of the cast and staff for making this story gloriously shine; the late Ms. Hiroko Matsuo and Ms. Kayoko Ito for introducing me to the Sakuramatsu in Kyoto and supporting me in my activities; Ms. Tomoko Ozawa and Ms. Kanae Kikuchi for their cooperation; my beloved parents up above; and the many people who supported me throughout this project. Thank you very much.

Spring, 2020

Waki Shiraishi

tality and dignity.

I have not included any illustrations as I wish for the readers to have the liberty of imagining, but I am hoping that something will reach the hearts of everyone who pick up this book, and bloom there.

Also, I wished to translate this story into English so more people could read it, and Mr. Yudai Mark Iwasaki, who is also a splendid actor, helped me make my wish come true. In this story, I did not specify the gender of the characters. Some genders may come to mind as the readers read, maybe from certain expressions or the way the characters speak, but I chose not to specify them because I believe what is really important is the inner traits of each character and their relationships. Mr. Iwasaki assented to this idea and reflected this in the translation. I am hoping you will enjoy how this story is presented in English, together with the Japanese.

Last but not least, I would like to thank Ms. Midori

gested that I recreate this story into a public musical reading. So, I rewrote it into a script with lyrics, and with the cooperation of director Mr. Kyoichi Itagaki, combined with Ms. Fukui's composition and musical performance, we put on a performance in October 2017. The venue was a café in Ryogoku, "black A." The cast members were Mr. Kohei Norizuki, Ms. Maho Minamoto, Mr. Takashika Kobayashi and Mr. "tekkan", and many people responded well to their performance. This performance certainly encouraged the publication of this original story. Also, I have reflected the performance a little bit in the revision.

The Sakuramatsu is still alive and healthy today, in April 2020, and has bloomed many beautiful flowers over the years. Even though twenty years have passed since it fell to the ground, its shape is still changing. Its bark is moss-grown, and each of the branches from the bark stretch high into the sky, now too high to reach even if you jump up. Inside, there is already a branch as thick as a second bark, and the tree is filled with indomitable vitree lying on the ground. Its bark was matsu, and its branches were sakura. Its flowers, which we would normally gaze up at, bloomed there beneath our feet, slightly glowing in the light, as if someone had scattered them on the ground. I finally understood what it was after Ms. Matsuo explained the story to me. A wild sakura seed had dropped inside the hollowed-out trunk of a matsu, spread its roots there, and grown. And this tree had fallen, with all its flowers in full bloom. The matsu was estimated to be 100 years old. The sakura was estimated to be 40 years old. I was standing there in the spring evening wind, heartbroken, and felt the urge that "I must write something," but I could not give it a shape at the moment. Since then, I spent ten years gradually spinning up this story. Greatly to my surprise, the Sakuramatsu, which I thought would not survive the collapse, revived splendidly over the years, while many people watched over it.

Then, after another ten years, in the spring of 2016, music maker Ms. Sayuri Fukui read this story and sug-

AFTERWORD

It was one night in April of 1996 that I met this extraordinary tree for the first time. That night, I was at a restaurant called Manharu, in Kamishichiken of Kyoto. Manharu was a French restaurant reformed from a tea house (traditionally a place for geiko-sans and maiko-sans, or geishas in Kyoto, to entertain patrons with their music and dance), and many people in the culture and art circles visited there. The restaurant was always filled with a warm supporting atmosphere for young promising people with a bright future. There, suddenly, someone who seemed to be a regular guest came in and said, "The matsu and sakura committed a double suicide." I must have had such a puzzled look on my face because the owner, Ms. Kayoko Ito insisted, "You should go and see for yourself." Ms. Hiroko Matsuo, a photographer, took me to Kyoto Gyoen, where this "Sakuramatsu" was. What I saw there was a sensational view. An uprooted

The sakura, who always had been the one embraced, was now embracing the matsu with its countless petals — graciously like an angel, and with the affection of a mother.

The wind chuckled, and breezily blew away a few of the petals.

And the wind decided to take off on its trip.

"Stay well."

The sakura answered,

"You too."

"Till next year."

"Yes, till next year."

Their voices echoed robustly in the spring skies.

"When the night finds the day!"

EPILOGUE

The wind shouted,

"It's the most magnificent petal storm in the world!"

The petals kept dancing in the wind.

They kept dancing,

And kept dancing,

Danced all the way into the sky,

Leaving an unforgettable view in the people's eyes,

And slowly, they floated down on top of the matsu.

And that moment, the matsu's posture from the morning after they first met crossed the wind's mind. The wind was starting to feel that it knew what the matsu wanted to see.

"Yes, that must be it."

The next morning.

The full moon carried the clouds away, and the sky was clear blue.

The wind knocked on the windows of the people who lived close by, and making sure they were open, glanced at the sakura and nodded. The sakura nodded back, closed its eyes, and entrusted itself completely to the wind.

The wind shot up the fresh petals into the sky with all its might.

A spray of light pink filled the blue sky.

It was the wildest dance of petals that anyone had ever seen.

"Can you see it?"

A person who came by to see the night sakura stopped and asked a companion.

"Yes, I see it's still very beautiful."

The wind poked the sakura.

"They just said, '*Still* beautiful.'"

The sakura shook its head in disappointment.

The companion answered.

"I see there's no wind today, so we can take our time to enjoy it."

Now the sakura whispered to the wind.

"They just said, 'Because there's *no* wind.'"

The wind stifled a laugh.

The two people heartily said,

"It encourages us to live on, doesn't it?"

"Yes, it certainly does."

A year had passed since that day.

Once again, the full moon had climbed high in the sky.

The wind, out of the blue, whispered these words,

"When the night finds the day..."

could feel its fluids regaining their warmth bit by bit, flowing through its body.

"I must live on."

And the sakura, determinedly, opened its eyes.

The sakura completely revived. Thanks to the people who covered its uprooted legs with soil, little by little, the scars in its body also began to heal.

The sakura survived through the summer, Persevered through the autumn, and endured the winter.

The wind was also always there. To encourage the sakura, the wind played the fool one time, tickled the sakura on another, and sometimes it just stood by the sakura silently. All just like the wind had done for the matsu before.

And the next spring, the sakura once again bloomed amazing flowers whilst lying on the ground.

"I see, so this is the famous 'SakuraMatsu?'"

"I must live on..."

The sakura thought, and weakly took a deep breath. A few of the buds, waiting to bloom, slightly opened.

The sakura stretched its arms. A severe pain shot through them, but the morning dew on the grass soothed the pain, and the smell of the dirt encouraged the sakura. It was a smell the sakura had forgotten for a while, from looking up at the sky too much. The sakura now remembered how it had always lived with its roots in this ground. The unforgettable pain from those final moments was not the only thing the sakura shared with the matsu. This ground was what had connected the sakura to the matsu for many years.

The warmth of the morning sun touched the flowers.

The sakura gently put a little strength into its body. Two of its petals slowly opened, as if shaking off the invisible arms that were holding them back.

The sakura gave its body another gentle push. Three more buds opened.

Another push. And now it was five buds. The sakura

The sakura, now alone, continued to gaze up at the sky for a while.

"When the night finds the day..."

Over and over, the sakura searched for the next words.

What had the matsu been trying to say?

If only the matsu had told me that.

The matsu's body was still there, wrapped around the sakura's body, but its warmth was gone. Everything just seemed like a dream.

"If only I could die now, together with the matsu..."

The sakura whispered to itself and was about to close its eyes, when it saw the light pink color of the flowers. The flowers bloomed there, not against the sky like always, but against the ground. The sakura could see that each and every flower was gently carrying a delicate soul.

The sakura gradually remembered the answers it had discovered to these questions through its year of contemplating—*Why was I given my life? Why am I here? What am I blooming my flowers every year for...?*

Episode 5　HEARTBEAT

"Listen! No matter how painful it is,

Don't avert your eyes.

Don't cover your ears.

Don't miss anything that happens on the earth and keep on telling the story.

Don't disappear when you should be there!"

"Why not?"

The storm replied quietly.

"Because that is what we are here for. That is what it means 'to be the wind.'

One day, you will also understand."

into tears.

The wind felt misery swelling in its heart.

If only I could also feel some pain in my body.

If only I could also wet the grass with my tears and stamp the ground with my feet.

I had spent a hundred years together with this irreplaceable friend, and we could never even talk again.

The wind turned around and flew all the way beyond the mountains, and burst out into a wild rage, on and on. The wind could not forgive itself for being who it was—born in the ancient fields and mountains where the dragons lived—with no body, no knowledge of pain, unable to shed any tears, and without an end to its life.

Suddenly the wind heard a voice.

"It's been a while, kid."

"You! What are you doing here?"

"It must be hard, isn't it?"

"Don't ask!"

The wind roared back at the storm, interrupting it. Then, the storm sharply scolded the wind.

ly stopped breathing.

Time went by...and the sakura opened its eyes to a white, misty morning. Birds were singing somewhere in the distance, and a few ants were crawling over its body. The wind was gently caressing the sakura's petals. Throughout the night, the wind had stayed there by the sakura's side.

"Are you awake?"

The wind asked, and the sakura asked in return in a raspy voice.

"What happened to...?"

The wind replied,

"Gone."

What more could be said?

And the wind knew these words would be irreversibly devastating if pondered upon.

The wind did not wait for them to take effect.

"Do your legs hurt?"

The sakura did not answer. Instead, it suddenly burst

heated body, tried to warm the matsu's body, which had always braced the sakura. The matsu leaned onto the sakura. It could feel the soft, rich, soothing touch of the sakura's bark, which it had embraced for so many years.

And like this, beneath the full moon, in full bloom, the two slowly, just so slowly, fell to the ground.

"The trees collapsed! The matsu and the sakura committed a double suicide!"

Rumors shot through the town. People gathered from all over and just stood there wordlessly. Light pink flowers bloomed profusely all over the ground. The flowers, slightly reflecting the pale moonlight, gave off a sweet scent. The people were utterly awed by the view.

The full moon watched over all this and slowly drifted across the sky.

Long moments went by, and one by one, the people walked away. The moon continued to light the matsu and the sakura, right until the moment the matsu quiet-

"This is..."

The moment this crack, an omen of a nightmare, reached the middle of its body, a fierce pain shot through the matsu. The matsu twisted its body in agony. The sakura's painful scream shot through the air. Their legs flipped up the dirt and rose into the air. For all that the matsu tried to hold its ground, it could not withstand the weight of the flowers. The matsu continued to fall over towards the ground.

The sakura tightly closed its eyes, bit down, and endured the pain while its legs slowly tore apart in different places.

"The time I had feared has come. It has come at last."

The sakura, trying to suppress its panic, repeatedly said to itself,

"Slowly, slowly. If we're going to fall, I have to slow it down so the matsu's body won't hit the ground too forcefully..."

The sakura pressed its cheek up against the matsu. The sakura rapidly circulated its fluids, and with its

A crisp full moon appeared in the sky.

The matsu, supporting the heavy weight with its whole body, gently cherished the sakura, and whispered in a low voice.

"How beautiful..."

The sakura, with its eyes closed, was enjoying the matsu's warmth.

The moon was high up in the sky.

The matsu looked up at the moon and the flowers and squinted as if they were too bright.

"Tomorrow will be sunny, too."

"Yes, tomorrow will be sunny."

It was quiet.

The matsu saw a certain dream-like view in its head, and started saying,

"When the night finds the day..."

It was that moment.

The matsu suddenly felt something unusual in its body. A single crack was slowly, just so slowly, creeping up its body.

The sakura, after regaining consciousness, went on day and night, pondering over one question: the meaning of its life.

Why was I given my life?

Why am I here?

What am I blooming my flowers every year for...?

The sakura could not put it into words, but it gradually began to feel something. It was a determination that welled up from deep within. This awareness made waking up every morning refreshing, fueled its daily life, and made sleep more soothing.

The next year, when spring came, the sakura bloomed splendidly beautiful flowers. It was so beautiful that the spring winds came all the way from the other mountains to take a look, and froze at the sight because it was so fascinatingly elegant.

The matsu watched over the sakura proudly.

The wind whispered to the matsu,

"It's amazing. There is no sakura like it."

Episode 4   THE FULL MOON

talk to me like that?"

"I'm stronger than you now. Just back off!"

The storm, laughing out loud, flew away into the distance.

The wind turned to see the matsu silently embracing the sakura. The matsu's hot fluids circulated through its body, trying to warm the exhausted sakura.

"Let's stay together."

Unable to say these three words, the matsu stood there silently, and embraced the sakura firmly.

trees lit up all in white, as if they had lost their colors.

Tonight, I am going to break myself into pieces. I am going to free the sakura as soon as I can.

When the lights finally pierced the sky above, the matsu opened its eyes wide and threw itself in to the light.

"Come on. I am not afraid. End this instantly!"

But the next moment...the matsu's heart froze. The sakura, who had woken up unnoticed, was stretching its neck out towards the storm, and spreading all of its branches to protect the matsu. Its young leaves were being torn off, and its slender branches were being blown away. The matsu called for the wind until its voice was lost.

When the wind arrived, the sakura was half unconscious. The wind expended all its power and pushed the storm away. The storm cursed, rolling its thunders.

"You idiot, I came because the matsu asked me to!"

The wind stood in front of the matsu and roared back.

"The matsu didn't really mean it, you half-wit!"

"You worthless kid, since when do you think you can

The sakura looked so painful. So the wind, reluctantly, blew away the newly bloomed petals. The petals, not yet in full bloom, scattered away in millions of directions, and the people who came to see the flowers were disappointed.

"Oh no, we couldn't make it in time."

"Oh well, the winds were strong."

The people regretfully stared at the wind.

The matsu gazed at these people silently. Then, it spoke to the sakura in a warm, relaxed voice that it had not spoken in for a very long time.

"Listen, have you ever thought about why you are alive?"

"..."

"Think about it. And never do anything like this again."

That night, the wind was traveling far when it heard an incredible sound. The matsu had called the storm. Lightning streaked through the skies, and fierce rain battered onto the ground. Beneath the strong lights, the

When the buds barely began to bloom, the sakura secretly called the wind whilst the matsu was sleeping.

"What's the matter?"

"I want to ask you a favor. Would you please scatter my petals?"

"What?! What are you saying? You just bloomed this morning."

"Just please."

The sakura stubbornly would not yield. It remembered the matsu's words. The matsu had said, the sakura's flowers were becoming heavier year by year.

The matsu said so as if it was happy, but it must have been burdensome to support my weight.

The sakura was convinced that this was the reason for the matsu's agony.

"It's probably just difficult for the matsu to tell me about it. But if I keep on like this, I will ruin the matsu's body. Please, do as I say."

"I can't do something like that."

"I beg you."

gone. Just imagining this tore the matsu's heart in half.

The matsu grimaced in agony and turned away from the sakura. Seeing the matsu like this, the sakura was frantically worried.

"Tell me what's wrong! Are you not feeling well? Are you hurt somewhere?"

The more the sakura clasped onto the matsu, the more the matsu was disturbed.

I know that I am responsible for confining you, yet I won't be able to live on without you...what should I do...?

These words came up to the tip of the matsu's tongue, but from there, they scattered into the air. The matsu was confused like it never had been before. But how could the sakura understand that? Embraced by the matsu's arms, which were now colder than ever, the sakura was in deep sorrow.

"We had understood each other so well..."

Because it was wounded so deeply, when spring came, the sakura buds seemed much paler than usual.

The matsu took a moment and studied the sakura carefully. For certain, its bark was exceptionally skinnier than the other sakuras.

Its delicate colors could be preserved only because it is mostly not in the sun. But it is obvious that the sakura wouldn't be able to live on its own. And surely this is my fault. Am I getting in the way of the sakura's future? A future that the sakura itself does not even know of?

The matsu thought,

"This isn't right,"

and felt its heart squeeze tight deep within.

"What's wrong?"

The sakura stopped singing and looked innocently into the matsu's face. But the matsu could not tell the sakura how it felt.

Yes, that's it. One day, somehow, I will have people transplant the sakura.

But this also meant that the sakura will disappear from the matsu's life. The sakura's laughing voice, its teasing small branches and smooth bark, its songs—all wind occasionally brought back. The sakura's voice was clear and beautiful, and the matsu's voice was filled with a warmth embracing every living thing in this world. Their duet, carried by the wind, echoed across the field and over the mountains, reaching faraway lands.

However—it was not long before the matsu's blissful heart was dimmed again by a new shadow. It was since the day the matsu heard a conversation between two people walking by.

"Is this the famous 'SakuraMatsu?'"

"It's amazing—so the bark is matsu and the branches sakura?"

"But the sakura seems a bit cramped, doesn't it?"

"If it stays like this, the sakura might not be able to grow any bigger."

Might not be able to grow any bigger...these words pierced through the matsu's heart. The matsu glanced at the sakura, but the sakura, utterly uninterested in this conversation, was looking up at the sky, humming.

The matsu reclaimed its former valiant figure. It did not have any more branches, but its bark firmly protected the sakura, shining brightly in the morning and evening sun.

The matsu taught various things to the sakura: that the sun rises in the east and sets in the west, that there were many different kinds of moons, about the constellations, the seasons, the animals...

The sakura, blessed with all this affection from the matsu, began to bloom beautiful flowers, and its branches became so nubile and graceful that they came to be called "the angel's arms."

The two trees' small bumps, slight tilts — everything fit together perfectly. They heard the voices of the same birds, they looked up at the same sky, they were together from the very moment they woke up until the moment they went to sleep, and they never felt distressed. They spoke to each other of every small detail until they ran out of words and fell asleep.

They composed many songs from the stories that the

Episode 3　LIGHT AND SHADOW

waved its arm towards the sun.

On another day, the sakura flickered new small leaves on its branches and tickled the matsu.

"Hey, hey," said the matsu. The sakura obliviously swayed its leaves and chuckled.

The wind watched over all this and thought to itself.

Now, the matsu will be okay without me. The matsu's bark had stopped withering. And the sakura is innocent and cheerful. Even without me there to make the matsu laugh, the matsu could be as happy as ever.

It would be lying for the wind to say it did not feel lonely. But the wind was happy enough that the matsu was able to redeem its former liveliness. Also, the wind now had important work to do. Year after year, more and more plants listened to the wind, and now all the seasonal changes in the area were conducted under the lead of the wind.

The wind gazed at the two of them, took a deep breath, and set out on its next job.

After pondering over this for many days, finally, the wind silently dropped a single seed inside the hollow of its friend.

The seed soon put forth its bud. Fortunately, with sunlight cheerfully pouring in through the open ceiling and holes on the side, and also blessed with plenty of rain, the bud soon grew into a sapling.

The matsu watched this sapling every day in amazement.

"Who are you?"

The matsu finally took a leap and asked, and then the sapling answered with a sweet voice, like a ringing bell.

"Sakura."

The sakura kept growing dynamically.

And on one beautiful morning, suddenly, the sakura swiftly reached out with its arm. The sakura's pliant arm slipped out of the holes in the matsu's body.

"Hey, hey," said the matsu. The sakura obliviously

"You can't do anything about it, it's my fate."

Hearing this, now it was the wind who blew out in anger.

"Stop acting cool, like you're okay!"

"..."

The matsu fell silent.

Since that day, the matsu closed its mind. Once closed, it did not open, no matter how many times, or how hard anyone knocked it. The wind learned that once something like this happened, the matsu's strength, which could even endure the storm, made it as stubborn as steel.

The matsu withered away day by day. Its needles dropped, its branches broke off, and still the matsu seemed to silently endure its fate.

How could I save the matsu's soul, its life?

How could I bring back the vigorous, refreshing matsu as it used to be?

How...? How could I...? How might I...?

"I'm empty!"

The matsu's voice gradually became louder.

"I'm empty. I'm totally empty! Do you understand what that feels like?!"

Needles dropped as the matsu hollered furiously. It was the first time that the wind saw the matsu like this. All the wind could do was tremble. And because the wind had no body, it could not easily say, "I understand." And being unable to say anything felt incredibly painful.

When the matsu calmed down a little, the wind mustered up its courage and asked in a small voice.

"Since when was this?"

"A little while ago."

"Why did it happen?"

"I don't know."

"Why didn't you tell me?"

"I couldn't. I couldn't tell you."

"What comes next?

"I become weaker and rot away."

"I don't want to watch you go through this."

Several decades went by. The wind and the matsu worked together and made this land very prosperous. Even though they clashed from time to time, they never despised each other. Even more, these fights helped them prepare for the storms that came from the other lands.

But there was one thing that the wind was not aware of. The matsu had begun holding a grave secret.

One day, the wind saw that the matsu was a little depressed. Meaning to cheer the matsu up, the wind playfully flirted with the matsu's arms. The wind had made its straight-minded friend laugh like this many times before. But on this day, the matsu's branch abruptly broke off. And the wind could not believe its eyes at what it saw the next moment. The matsu had grown to become a big tree, but beneath its bark, its insides had decayed into a huge hollow.

"What is this?"

The matsu dropped its shoulders heavily and moaned in a hoarse voice.

Episode 2　SAKURA

"The other trees won't stir for you?"

"No, all they do is just sway foolishly. They're so arrogant. They don't really accept me."

"I see. Okay. Let's try it out now."

The wind danced a light breeze, and the matsu swayed its firm branches and stirred its needles skillfully.

The wind was astonished because the matsu understood everything the wind was feeling.

"How could you understand me like that?"

"I don't know. I could just feel it."

The matsu was also feeling an empathy for the wind, like they had known each other for a very long time.

So, this is how the matsu came to stir its branches for the wind, and the wind came to bring the matsu news of the weather and changing seasons, and stories of what was going on elsewhere in the world. And both of them grew to become especially acknowledged by the surrounding trees and plants.

The wind said from its heart.

"Oh, I'm still nothing."

The matsu laughed and answered casually. The matsu stood there resolutely, not even scarcely seeming to reproach the wind for smashing into it last night. Even more, the matsu honestly admired how the wind could fly around anywhere it wanted to.

"I envy you, pal. You can go anywhere."

These words aroused a curious feeling within the wind. In this matsu's voice, the wind could hear an affection that it had never felt before in any other tree. Even abruptly being called "pal" made the wind feel happy.

The wind answered.

"If it's stories of the world you want, I will bring as many as you like. With a bit of time, I can even fly to the other side of the Earth. In return, can I ask you a favor? Will you…give me a shape? Nobody knows that I exist unless someone stirs in my wind. No matter how much I jump or shout, whatever I do, I just end up with the storm bringing a fight on me like last night."

It was a long long time ago, when the matsu and the wind first met.

Back then, the wind had still been very restless, nor did it have any intentions of resting. Day after day, the wind would go around wooing small flowers with its gentle breeze just to casually slip away—and the wind had thought that was all there was to its life. It was just one such spring night that the wind, caught in a fight with a gigantic storm and shoved away, smashed into this young matsu.

The matsu caught this crashing wind with its slender body without budging. It did not scatter any of its needles or bits of its bark, nor did it break any of its branches.

Next morning, when all the other trees were exhausted from the night-long storm, the matsu alone stood there with its back stretched straight up towards the bright morning sun. It was a view so brisk that the wind had never seen before.

"You are amazing."

Episode 1   THE ENCOUNTER

The wind that blows in spring—
        The east skylark wind,
The wind that a dragon starts—
        The swift spring storm,
Come tailwind,
        So quickly can you run—
Come headwind,
        So far can you fly—
When the wind subsides,
Let us look up to the sky,
And drift our minds away
To that very special day.

PROLOGUE

CONTENTS

The story of sakura, a Japanese cherry blossom, and matsu, a Japanese pine tree, and the wind and the storm.

SakuraMatsu
When the night finds the day

A story by Waki Shiraishi

Translated by Yudai Mark Iwasaki

本書への感想は以下のURLかQRコードからも
お送りいただけます。
https://forms.gle/VU4AY27sMsuMxoJp8

NDC913
神奈川　銀の鈴社　2020
100頁　18.8cm（さくらまつ ──夜が明けたら──）

銀鈴叢書

さくらまつ ──夜が明けたら──

2020年9月2日　初版発行
本体1,500円＋税

著　者　　白石　和己 ©
英　訳　　岩崎 MARK 雄大 ©
発行者　　柴崎聡・西野真由美
発行所　　㈱銀の鈴社
　　　　　〒248-0017　鎌倉市佐助1-10-22　佐助庵
　　　　　TEL 0467-61-1930　FAX 0467-61-1931
　　　　　https://www.ginsuzu.com

©Waki Shiraishi　©Yudai Mark Iwasaki　Printed in Japan

ISBN 978-4-86618-095-3 C0093
落丁・乱丁本はお取替え致します
印刷　電算印刷／製本　渋谷文泉閣